C463644220

LUCY DANIELS

h
*Hodder
Children's
Books*

A division of Hachette Children's Books

To Molly and Thomas

Special thanks to Linda Chapman

Little Animal Ark is a trademark of Working Partners Limited
Text copyright © 2001 Working Partners Limited
Created by Working Partners Limited, London, W6 0QT
Illustrations copyright © 2001 Andy Ellis

First published in Great Britain in 2001 by Hodder Children's Books

This edition published in 2007

The rights of Lucy Daniels and Andy Ellis to be identified as the author
and illustrator of this work respectively have been asserted by them in
accordance with the Copyright, Designs and Patents Act 1988.

4

A Catalogue record for this book is available from the
British Library

ISBN-13: 978 0 340 93255 1

Printed and bound in Great Britain by Clays Ltd, St Ives plc

Hodder Children's Books
A division of Hachette Children's Books
338 Euston Road, London NW1 3BH
An Hachette Livre UK Company

Chapter One

"Your turn now, Mandy!" Mr Simkins called. He helped a boy off Sparky's back.

Mandy Hope ran over, her heart thumping with excitement. It was her friend Sarah Drummond's eighth birthday party. Sarah's mum had asked Mr Simkins to bring Sparky the Party Pony, to give rides in the garden.

"Hello, Sparky," Mandy said.

She stroked the pony's neck.

Sparky turned to look at her.
His pale forelock fell over his eyes
like a very long fringe.

"Are you looking forward to your ride, Mandy?" Mr Simkins asked, smiling at her. Mandy knew him well because his daughter, Pippa, was in the same class as her at school.

"Oh, yes!" Mandy said. Ever since she had heard that Sparky was coming to the party, she had been able to think about only one thing – having a ride on him. She loved animals. Her mum and dad were both vets, and Mandy had decided that one day, she would like to be a vet too.

Mr Simkins handed her a riding hat. Mandy squashed it eagerly onto her short blonde hair.

"Now, hold onto the saddle and I'll help you up," Mr Simkins said.

Mandy reached up for the saddle. A second later she was sitting on Sparky's back.

She gathered up the reins and gripped his sides with her knees.

Mr Simkins clicked his tongue and Sparky began to walk up the garden.

Mandy could see her friends playing, but she didn't want to be anywhere else but here on Sparky's back. A gentle breeze blew on her face as his smooth stride carried her across the grass. She breathed in the pony's warm scent of hay and leather.

"I think all parties should have pony rides!" she said happily.

Mr Simkins smiled. "Sparky would like that. He loves being a party pony."

Sparky tossed his head as if he agreed.

Mandy laughed. "When's his next party, Mr Simkins?" she asked.

"Next weekend," Mr Simkins said. "But we won't have to travel very far," he added, smiling. "It's Pippa's birthday! She's bringing the party invitations to school on Monday. I think she's inviting your whole class."

"Oh, great!" Mandy said. "Did you hear that, boy?" she told Sparky. "I'll get to ride you again next weekend!"

They reached the end of the garden. Mr Simkins turned Sparky round. "Would you like to trot?" he asked Mandy.

"Yes, please!" she said.

"Trot on!" Mr Simkins said to Sparky. And the pony slid into a trot.

At first, it felt a bit bumpy to Mandy. But soon she was rising up and down in the saddle, in time with Sparky's quick, bouncy strides.

Mandy wished the ride could go on for ever and ever. But soon they got back to the starting point and it was someone else's turn.

Mr Simkins helped Mandy to get off.

"Thank you," she said, giving Sparky a hug.

The pony nudged her with his soft muzzle.

Mandy handed over the
riding hat, then went to find
Pippa.

She found her over by the present table. "Pippa, your dad says you're having a party next weekend," she said eagerly.

Pippa nodded, and her blonde ponytail bounced up and down. "On Saturday. It's going to be a

pony party!" she said, her eyes shining. "I'm going to have a pony-shaped cake! And Dad's going to give everyone loads of rides on Sparky, of course! You will come, won't you?"

"You bet!" Mandy said happily. She looked at Sparky, setting off with another guest on his back and sighed. "You're so lucky to have a pony, Pippa."

"I know," Pippa said. "Mum and Dad bought Sparky for me last Christmas. He was quite expensive, so he's a Christmas and birthday present combined. But now I've got him I don't care if I *never* have another present!"

Mandy looked wistfully at the brown pony. She was sure she'd feel the same. "I wish I had a pony," she said. "I'd love to look after one."

"Would you like to come and help me get Sparky ready for my party next Saturday?" Pippa said suddenly.

"Like to?" Mandy gasped in delight. "I'd love to!"

Chapter Two

Mandy could hardly wait for next weekend. And at last, Saturday morning arrived. "It's time to go!" she said, hopping up and down on the spot. "Come on, Mum!"

But Emily Hope, Mandy's mum, seemed determined to take her time. "Now have you got your party clothes to change into?" she asked calmly.

"Yes!" Mandy said.

"And Pippa's present?" her mum said.

"Yes!" Mandy cried. The day before, she had been to Piper's Pets, the pet shop in Walton. She'd chosen a smart red lead rope for Sparky. It was carefully wrapped in her bag. *"Please* can we go, Mum?" she begged.

Emily Hope smiled. "OK then. Go and get in the Land-rover."

They set off through the village of Welford. Pippa and her family lived just outside the village in an old house. It had a large rambling garden and a paddock just the right size for a pony.

Pippa came running out of the house before Mrs Hope had even stopped the Land-rover.

"Have a good time," Mrs Hope said as Mandy jumped out.

"We will! Bye, Mum!" Mandy called. She waved to her mum and then followed Pippa inside.

Mrs Simkins was standing at the large kitchen table making some sandwiches.

"Hi, Mrs Simkins," Mandy said. Then she spotted an enormous cake on the side. It was made in the shape of a pony. "Wow!" she gasped. She went over to look more closely. The cake was covered in chocolate icing, and it had a shaggy white icing mane and tail.

"Isn't it brilliant?" said Pippa. "Mum made it. And she made these, too." She showed Mandy a tray of home-made cookies. Each had a pony head drawn with icing on top. There was also a tray of jellies in pony-shaped paper dishes.

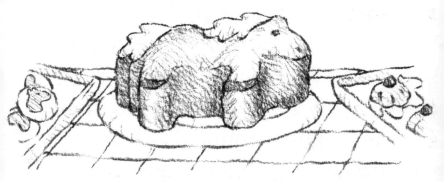

Mandy thought it all looked wonderful.

Mrs Simkins smiled. "Go and look in the garden," she said.

Mandy ran outside with Pippa. Mr Simkins was decorating the trees and hedges with rows and rows of rainbow-coloured paper horseshoes. Along one side of the garden was a big banner that said, *Pippa's Pony Party!*

"Everything at the party is about ponies," Pippa said proudly to Mandy. "And now we've got to make Sparky look really perfect."

Mr Simkins overheard them. "You'd better go and get him in from the field then, girls," he said. "He could probably do with a good brush."

Mandy and Pippa went down the path that led from the garden to Sparky's paddock. As they reached the gate they saw that Sparky was cantering around his field. Suddenly he put his head down and kicked up his heels, over and over again.

Pippa stared in surprise. "He doesn't usually do that," she said.

"Maybe he's just feeling frisky," Mandy said.

Pippa untied Sparky's leadrope from the gate. "Sparky!" she called, going into the field.

The pony tossed his head and trotted over.

Mandy patted his neck. He nuzzled her for a moment and then swung his head round and stared at his left side.

Pippa pulled Sparky's leadrope. "Come on, Sparky. It's time for you to be groomed." She led Sparky up to his wooden stable.

Next to the stable was a large shed. "This is where we keep his feed, riding tack and other stuff," Pippa said. She tied Sparky up outside. "I'll get his grooming kit."

While Pippa went into the shed, Mandy stayed outside with Sparky.

The pony snuffled her hands.

Mandy smiled. "Hello, boy," she whispered, stroking his face.

Sparky's eyes peeped at her from under his shaggy forelock. He swished his long, thick tail. It was full of tangles and his coat was covered with dust from where he had been lying down in the field.

Pippa came out of the shed with a plastic box filled with brushes. "We start by using the dandy brushes," she said. She took out two hard-bristled brushes and handed one to Mandy. "They'll get all the mud and dust out of his coat. That's the most important bit."

Mandy started on the left side and Pippa on the right. Mandy brushed as hard as she could.

Great clouds of dust flew up from Sparky's neck and shoulder.

But as she swept the dandy brush over his side, he suddenly threw his head up and jumped as if he was in pain.

Mandy put the dandy brush down and looked more closely at where she had been brushing. She saw a swollen lump on Sparky's left side, just where his saddle went. It was about the size of Mandy's palm. "Look, Pippa!"  she gasped. "He's hurt himself!"

Pippa hurried round to Mandy's side. Mandy gently touched the lump. It was hot and when she touched it, Sparky flinched.

Pippa looked very worried. "I wonder what it is? We'd better get my dad!"

Chapter Three

Mr Simkins was balancing on a ladder, tying some pink streamers to one of the apple trees.

"Dad!" Pippa shouted, as she and Mandy ran up the garden. "Sparky's hurt himself!"

"Hurt himself?" Mr Simkins said. He climbed down the ladder. "What do you mean?"

"There's a big lump on his side," said Mandy.

"Come quick!" Pippa begged.
Mr Simkins followed Mandy
and Pippa to where Sparky was
tied up.

The pony lifted his head and whinnied as they all hurried down the path towards him. He looked very sorry for himself.

Pippa pointed out the lump. "Mandy found it when we were grooming him," she said.

Mandy watched as Mr Simkins gently felt the swelling on Sparky's back. "What's he done, Mr Simkins?" she asked, feeling very worried.

"I don't know." Mr Simkins frowned as Sparky flinched. "Maybe his saddle's been rubbing him. I'd better call Animal Ark and see if your mum or dad can come and take a look, Mandy."

Pippa put her arms around Sparky's neck. "Oh, poor Sparky," she said. She looked as if she might cry.

"I'll go and ring straight away," Mr Simkins said, and he hurried off.

*

Fifteen minutes later, Emily Hope arrived.

"Mum!" Mandy called, running over as her mum came down to the paddock with Mr Simkins.

"Hello, love," Mrs Hope said. "I hear Sparky's been in the wars. Let's have a look, then."

Pippa pointed out the lump. "It wasn't there yesterday," she said shakily.

Mrs Hope examined the swelling.

"Do you know what it is, Mum?" Mandy asked anxiously.

Her mum looked up and nodded. "It's a bee sting," she said. She smiled reassuringly. "It's nothing to worry about."

Mandy let out her breath. So Sparky wasn't badly hurt! She looked at Pippa and saw a look of relief on her friend's face.

"A bee sting!" Mr Simkins said in surprise. "I didn't know bees stung horses."

"It is quite unusual," said Mrs Hope. "He must have been stung when he was out in his field."

Mandy clutched Pippa's arm as she remembered something. "He was bucking when we went to catch him, wasn't he?"

Pippa nodded. "Yes! He was cantering round! Maybe he'd just been stung."

"That sounds likely," agreed Mrs Hope. She opened her black veterinary bag. "I'll just take the sting out and give you some cream for him."

Then she turned to look at everyone. "I'm sorry," she said, "but Sparky shouldn't be ridden for a few days."

Mandy gasped. What about the party? She looked at Pippa. Her friend looked very upset.

"You do understand, don't you, Pippa?" asked Mrs Hope. "Sparky can't wear a saddle until the swelling's gone right down. He can still go to your party but he can't be ridden. We don't want his side to get worse."

Pippa bit her lip, then she nodded. "I understand," she whispered.

Mandy sighed. Poor Pippa! And poor Sparky!

Chapter Four

"It's so unfair," Pippa said, when her dad and Mrs Hope had left.

She sat down in the doorway of the shed and buried her face in her knees.

Mandy sat down beside her. She wished there was something she could say to comfort her friend. "Sparky can still come to the party," she said. "He won't have to miss out."

"But it won't be the same,"
Pippa said, sadly. "Sparky loves
giving rides. He won't understand
why he hasn't got his saddle on."

Mandy looked up at Sparky. He stamped his foot and whinnied at them as if to say, *What's happening? Why are you sitting down?*

Mandy got up. "Poor boy," she said. She went over and patted him. "At least your back is going to be all right." She looked at Pippa. "Shall I carry on grooming him?" she asked, not knowing what else to do. "Even though he can't give rides, we can still make him look nice."

Pippa nodded and stood up. "You're right," she said, and picked up a brush, too.

Sparky nuzzled her arm.

He seemed to sense that his owner was unhappy.

"Oh, Sparky," Pippa said. "Why did you have to get stung?"

Mandy and Pippa groomed in silence. At long last, all the dust and mud was out of Sparky's coat.

"Should we start washing his tail?" Mandy asked, putting her brush away in the grooming box.

Pippa nodded. "There's a bucket in the shed."

Mandy went into the shed. The plastic buckets were piled up in a corner next to a couple of metal feed-bins. The other side of the barn was filled with bales of hay and straw.

Suddenly Mandy stopped and stared. Among the bales was something that looked like a dusty old pony cart. Hanging on a nail nearby, was a leather harness.

Mandy went closer. The paint on the wood was peeling, but the cart looked like it might still work!

Just then, Pippa came into the shed. "Have you found a bucket?" she asked. Then she saw Mandy looking at the cart. "Oh, that's Sparky's," she said. "His last owners gave it to us when we bought him. It's quite old, but Dad keeps saying that he's going to paint it one day."

"Does Sparky know how to pull it?" Mandy asked.

"Oh, yes," said Pippa. "His last owners trained him."

An idea burst into Mandy's head. "Pippa!" she gasped. "Why don't we clean the cart up today?"

"Why?" Pippa asked, puzzled.

"Because then Sparky could *pull* everyone round for rides!" Mandy said. "Sparky wouldn't have to wear a saddle, and everyone would love it!"

Pippa's eyes lit up. "You really think so?"

"Yes!" Mandy said. "Pippa, it would be brilliant!"

Chapter Five

Mandy and Pippa ran to find Mr
Simkins. He was putting out some
wooden tables in the garden.

He looked round as Mandy
and Pippa raced up the path
towards him. "You two look in a
hurry! Where's the fire?"

"There isn't a fire, Dad,"
gasped Pippa. "But Mandy's just
had a really good idea. You know
that old cart . . ."

She gabbled out Mandy's idea. "What do you think?" she finished.

Mandy looked hopefully at Pippa's dad.

"Well . . ." said Mr Simkins, frowning thoughtfully. "We'll have to check that the harness doesn't touch the sting on Sparky's back, of course. And it'll be a fair bit of work making the cart look presentable. But it might just work! Good thinking, Mandy."

Mandy and Pippa hugged each other in delight.

They went to the shed and Mr Simkins fetched the harness.

Sparky looked quite surprised

to have it placed on his back. He
turned his head and sniffed at the
leather as Mr Simkins did up the
buckles.

"It doesn't touch his sting at all," Mandy said happily.

"No, it should be fine," Mr Simkins said, looking pleased. "It will need a good clean though."

"We'll do that!" Pippa said. "Come on, Mandy!"

While Mr Simkins took the cart out of the shed and checked it over, Mandy and Pippa sat down with some water and saddle soap.

Pippa showed Mandy how to soap the leather to make it clean and soft. "It's lucky you came round early," she said. "There's loads to do."

Mandy nodded. "We've got to finish this and wash Sparky's mane and tail . . ."

"And then make the cart look good," Pippa said, smiling happily.

"Well, it seems to be in working order," Mr Simkins called to them from the cart. "I'll give it a good dust down, then you can decorate it. There are some more streamers in the house. Maybe you could use those."

Mandy and Pippa worked as quickly as they could. They finished the harness and washed Sparky's tail. And when they ran into the house to get the streamers, they told Pippa's mum all about their idea.

Mrs Simkins fetched them some ribbons to attach to the cart, too. "I can't wait to see it when it's finished!" she said. "But you'd better be quick. There's

only an hour before the guests
start to arrive."

Mandy and Pippa raced back
to the cart and began to attach
the rainbow-coloured streamers.
They wound them all round the
cart. Then they tied the ribbons
in bows all along the top rail.
There were also a few ribbons left
for the harness.

Sparky watched them. He
stamped his front hoof and tossed
his head excitedly. He seemed to
know that he was going to pull
his cart again.

"There!" Mandy said at last,
standing back.

"Wow!" Pippa cried.

The cart looked completely different. Its shabby paintwork was hidden by the pretty decorations that fluttered in the breeze. Bright ribbons were tied in bows, all over Sparky's harness.

"It looks brilliant!" Mandy said happily.

Just then, they heard Mrs Simkins calling down the garden. "Mandy! Pippa! There's only ten minutes to go!"

Giving Sparky one last pat, Mandy and Pippa raced up to the house.

"Look at the state of you!" Mrs Simkins exclaimed as they ran into the kitchen.

Mandy caught sight of
herself in the kitchen mirror.
Her clothes were covered with
dust, and her hair was sticking up.

But she didn't care. Sparky
and the cart were ready for the
party, and that was all that
mattered.

Mandy and Pippa only just had time to wash and change into their clean clothes.

Soon the doorbell began to ring as the guests arrived.

"Right, if you'd all like to come through to the garden," Mrs Simkins said, when everyone was there.

Everyone trundled out – and gasped in surprise.

The horseshoe banners were draped between the trees. The wooden tables were piled high with the sandwiches, cakes and jellies that Mrs Simkins had made. But what made people stand and stare the most was Sparky.

Mr Simkins was holding the pony in the middle of the garden. Behind him was the cart.

Mandy smiled to herself. It didn't look anything like the dusty old object that Mandy had first seen in the shed. Mr Simkins had added some stripy red cushions to the seats, and the bows and streamers fluttered merrily.

When Sparky saw Mandy and Pippa he lifted his head and whinnied proudly as if to say, *Look at me!*

"Oh wow!" one of the guests cried, looking at the cart. "Are we all going to have a ride in it?"

"Of course," Mr Simkins said with a smile. He raised his voice. "Let the pony party begin!"

Mandy thought that this was the best birthday party ever! There were lots of party games with prizes and the food was delicious and fun.

But what everyone liked best was riding round the garden in Sparky's cart.

Sparky seemed to be having a lovely time too. He nuzzled everyone who patted and stroked him.

And Pippa's mum had prepared a special plate of apple and carrot pieces for him.

Just before it was time to go home, Mr Simkins organised a photograph. Everyone crowded around Pippa and Sparky and the cart.

"Mandy!" Pippa called. "Come and stand at the front!"

Mandy went and stood on the other side of Sparky. "It's been a brilliant party," she said, her eyes shining.

"Thanks to your idea," said Pippa.

Sparky pushed his head against her, as if to say, *What about me?*

"And to Sparky, of course!" Mandy laughed, giving him a hug.

Read more about Animal Ark in The Lucky Lamb

Chapter One

"Dad, is it time for my surprise now?" Mandy Hope asked eagerly. She finished her apple pie and custard, and put down her spoon. "I've been waiting for ages!"

Mr Hope laughed. "Just let me finish my pudding, Mandy!" he said.

"Mandy's going to burst if she doesn't find out what the surprise is soon," Mrs Hope said with a smile.

"I'm so full, I think I *might* burst!" Mandy joked, patting her tummy. "That was a lovely lunch. Thanks, Gran."

Mandy and her mum and dad were having Sunday lunch with Gran and Grandad Hope. On the way to Lilac Cottage, Mr Hope had told Mandy that he had a surprise for her. She couldn't wait to find out what it was. All she knew was that they would have to go in the Land-rover.

Mandy hoped it was something to do with animals. Mandy *loved* animals! Her mum and dad were vets at Animal Ark, and Mandy wanted to be a vet too one day.

"Anyone for seconds?" her gran asked. She picked up the jug of custard.

"Not for me, thanks," Mr Hope said. "I'd better not keep Mandy waiting any longer!"